Property of
Teacher Resource Room
Bundy - Room 429
Santa Monica College
310-434-3316

P9-BIP-074

**Purchased Through
CAREER FUNDS**

Edie

Morningtown Ride

Words and Music by Malvina Reynolds   **Illustrations by Michael Leeman**

THE CROSSING PRESS
FREEDOM, CA

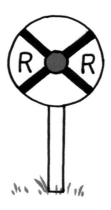

Copyright © 1984 by Michael J. Leeman
Morningtown Ride song, copyright © Amadeo Music 1962
Published originally in 1984 by Turn the Page Press.
Published in a new edition by The Crossing Press in 1996, reprinted with permission.

Cover and interior design by Victoria May
Printed in Hong Kong

Cataloging-in-Publication Data available
ISBN 0-89594-763-3

for Meghan

Special thanks to Carrie, Bev, and the Bos Family Singers for their constant encouragement.

Train whistle blowing,
makes a sleepy noise,

Underneath their blankets
go all the girls and boys,

Heading from the station, out along the bay,

All bound for Morningtown,
many miles away.

Sarah's at the engine,

Tony rings the bell,

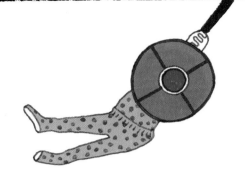

John swings the lantern
to show that all is well,

Rocking, rolling, riding
out along the bay,

All bound for Morningtown,
many miles away.

Maybe it is raining
where our train will ride,

But all the little travelers
are snug and warm inside.

Somewhere there is sunshine, somewhere there is day,

Somewhere there is Morningtown, many miles away.

Morningtown Ride

words and music by Malvina Reynolds

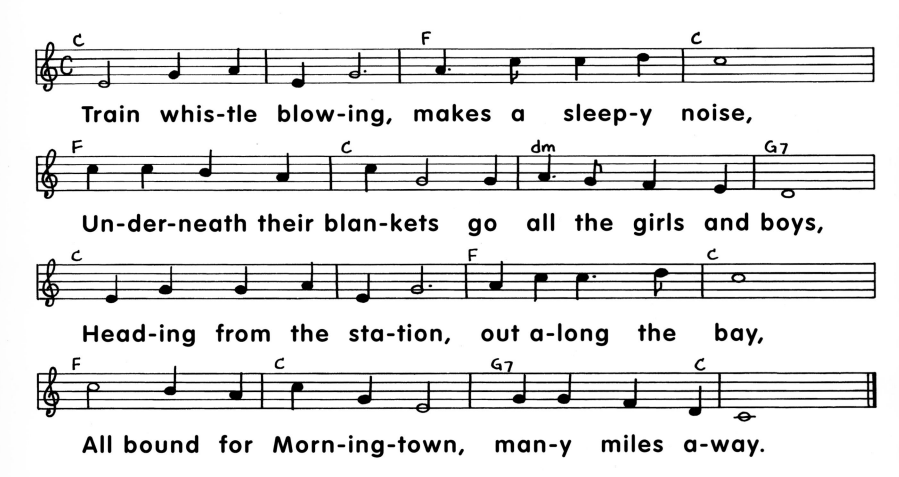

Train whis-tle blow-ing, makes a sleep-y noise,

Un-der-neath their blan-kets go all the girls and boys,

Head-ing from the sta-tion, out a-long the bay,

All bound for Morn-ing-town, man-y miles a-way.

© Amadeo Music 1962

Sarah's at the engine,
   Tony rings the bell,

John swings the lantern
   to show that all is well,

Rocking, rolling, riding
   out along the bay,

All bound for Morningtown,
   many miles away.

Maybe it is raining
   where our train will ride,

But all the little travelers
   are snug and warm inside.

Somewhere there is sunshine,
   somewhere there is day,

Somewhere there is Morningtown,
   many miles away.

The Crossing Press
publishes children's books.
Please write for a listing
or call 1-800-777-1048.